Becky flattened her... hardly daring to breathe. If there was new glass in the porthole, someone had put it there, and put it there for a reason. And that someone might be around, might even be inside the house-boat now! With a thumping heart, she edged nearer the porthole and forced herself to take a quick look inside.

Becky's sailing holiday with her family looks as if it will be quite dull, until the Fielding family turn up. But why are they so distant and unfriendly? Even Jake, their son, is on edge. Then Becky's sister goes missing, and the need to solve the mystery becomes urgent.

Rosemary Hayes' first career was in advertising. Then she spent several years in Australia, where she took a writing course at Monash University. Her first novel, *Race Against Time*, was runner-up for the Kathleen Fidler Award. Rosemary Hayes now runs a small publishing company in Cambridgeshire, where she lives with her husband, their three children and a great many animals.

By the same author

DREAMCHILD
RACE AGAINST TIME

Rosemary Hayes

SEAL CRY

Illustrated by Laszlo B. Acs

PUFFIN BOOKS

For Eve

PUFFIN BOOKS

Published by the Penguin Group
Penguin Books Ltd, 27 Wrights Lane, London W8 5TZ, England
Penguin Books USA Inc., 375 Hudson Street, New York, New York 10014, USA
Penguin Books Australia Ltd, Ringwood, Victoria, Australia
Penguin Books Canada Ltd, 10 Alcorn Avenue, Toronto, Ontario, Canada M4V 3B2
Penguin Books (NZ) Ltd, 182–190 Wairau Road, Auckland 10, New Zealand

Penguin Books Ltd, Registered Offices: Harmondsworth, Middlesex, England

First published by Blackie and Son Ltd 1991
Published in Puffin Books 1993
1 3 5 7 9 10 8 6 4 2

Chapter One

Becky crouched beneath the wooden bridge. In one hand she held a fishing net and in the other a long piece of string, weighted with a stone. The string, with a piece of meat on the end, sank slowly down and settled near the bottom of the creek. The tide was dropping, and black mud oozed between her toes, but Becky took no notice. Her eyes never left the string as it moved gently to and fro, disturbed only by the pull of the water on its way out to sea.

Several minutes passed. She kept absolutely still. She didn't hear the gulls screaming above her or the clink-clink of wire against the metal masts of the moored dinghies. She had seen the big crab again. The one she'd been trying to catch all afternoon. He was down there in the muddy water, moving sideways, very slowly, towards the string.

Then, at last, she felt the sudden tug which

meant that the crab had taken the bait. Becky leant forward and with a swift, smooth movement, pulled up the string and scooped the fishing net underneath.

Still crouching, she peered into the net and grinned. Then she got to her feet carefully, so as not to slip on the mud, and looked up. 'I've got him!' she shouted. 'Look!'

Her father was leaning over the bridge. He smiled down at her. 'Let's see. Bring him up here.'

Becky plopped the huge crab into a bucket of sea water with the smaller crabs she'd caught and slithered her way up the bank to the bridge.

Dad looked at the crab, which was scrabbling and splashing in the bucket. 'He's a monster! A great-grandfather crab!'

Becky smoothed her hair back from her forehead with a muddy hand. 'He's the biggest I've ever caught!'

She put the bucket down on the bridge and stretched, cramped from squatting in one position for so long. Dad put his arm round her shoulders and they stood together on the bridge, watching the last dinghies sail in from the harbour before the water dropped too far.

For as long as she could remember, Becky had been here for holidays. She loved the creeks and the marshland and everything to do with boats and the sea. She'd always been happy here, crabbing and sailing and walking and swimming. But this time it was different.

7

This time there was no-one to share it all. Becky's sister, Emma, was grown up and didn't come on holiday with them any more.

Dad shifted his arm and bent down to pick up the bucket. He must have read her thoughts. 'This morning I was talking to the man who runs the new sailing school,' he said. 'He's called Jim Fielding and I think he's got children. Maybe you could ask them to sail with you.'

Becky looked down the big creek to where their dinghy was moored. Even from the bridge she could see its name, *Myrtle*, proud against the white paint of the stern. 'Oh, I don't know, Dad. If they run a sailing school, they wouldn't think much of old *Myrtle*.'

Dad smiled. '*Myrtle* may be old,' he said. 'But she's solid and reliable. A good family boat.'

Becky made a face. She longed for something more racy, and imagined herself skimming across the harbour in a Topper or a Laser.

'Come on,' said Dad. 'We'll put these crabs back and then we'll go and look for the Fieldings.' Together they released the crabs at the top of the muddy bank and watched them scuttle and slide back to freedom in the water.

It didn't take long to find the Fieldings. Boats could only go out from the creek when the water was high, so sailing lessons had just finished for the day.

The whole family was there. A man and a woman, a boy of about Becky's age, stocky and dark, and a much older girl, probably in her late teens or early twenties, with a slim figure and long dark hair which hung over her face as she worked.

The man was giving change to some customers while the woman and the boy and girl were busy taking down sails, putting on covers, and generally making the boats safe and secure until lessons started again tomorrow.

Becky felt shy, and she hung back while her father went closer.

'Good afternoon!'

The man continued to chat to his customers, but the woman stopped what she was doing and looked up. She shielded her eyes to see better. 'Good afternoon,' she replied, but her voice was muffled by the sound of flapping

sails and the chugging of a passing motorboat.

'I met your husband earlier,' said Dad, raising his voice so that it carried across the water.

The woman said nothing; Dad went on. 'I was wondering if your children would like to use our boat sometimes, when you and your husband are giving lessons? It's a sturdy dinghy and it would be company for my daughter.'

There was an awkward silence and Becky blushed. Why did Dad blunder in like this? He always thought people would agree with his ideas. She looked at him, smiling across at the Fieldings, then she glanced at the boy. He had heard Dad's voice and was moving nearer in order to hear better. For a moment, his eyes met Becky's, then they both looked away and the boy went back to wind the mainsail round the boom.

'Er…I don't know,' began the woman, 'It's just that…'

Then a man's voice cut in from the bank. It was Jim Fielding. 'No, I'm afraid that's out of the question. My children have to help here during the season. We're very busy. And Penny teaches as well as my wife and myself.'

Becky felt sorry for her father as he shrugged his shoulders and gave an embarrassed smile. 'Oh…well…yes, I see. Yes of course they must help you. I'm sorry.'

The boy and the girl had stopped working and a glance passed between them. Then the girl – Penny – spoke, and her voice was cool. 'Jake doesn't teach, Dad. Only three of us teach. He has plenty of spare time.'

There was an uneasy silence while father and daughter stared at each other across the water, then Jim Fielding dropped his gaze. 'There's a lot he can do on shore,' he mumbled.

'He's only fourteen, Dad. He ought to have *some* fun!'

There was another long silence, broken only by the ever-present sound of boats and water. Becky felt that, without realising it, she and Dad had stirred up a family row and she wanted to creep away and not get involved.

Then, quite suddenly, Jim Fielding changed his mind. 'All right,' he said, gruffly. 'I suppose he could do with a break. Not every day, though. I can't spare him every day.'

For the first time, Jake spoke. 'Which is your dinghy?' he asked Becky.

'The *Myrtle*, the white Gull moored over there,' said Becky, pointing.

Jake nodded and smiled. 'I'll be there tomorrow, as soon as our boats have gone out.'

Jim Fielding looked briefly at *Myrtle*, then he turned to Jake and their eyes met. There was a moment of silent communication between them before Jim Fielding said. 'Be careful.'

He had spoken very softly, but the words were clear and Becky heard them. She looked up sharply. Jake must be a good sailor so why was Jim Fielding worried about him sailing in old *Myrtle*? Then she saw that the whole family were looking at Jake, waiting for his reply, and

Becky sensed the tense atmosphere between them.

'I'll take care,' said Jake, and his face was serious.

Becky and Dad left then, but as they walked across the quay, Becky frowned to herself. There was something strange in the way Jim Fielding had said 'Be careful'. It was as if he was warning Jake. But if he *was* warning him, he certainly wasn't warning him of the dangers of sailing in *Myrtle*.

Chapter Two

It was mid-afternoon the next day before the tide was high enough to sail out from the creek. Becky walked down to where *Myrtle* was moored and started to take off the cover and set up the rigging. Every now and again she glanced towards the sailing school where several people were waiting for lessons. There were two Fielding boats going out today and Becky watched as they passed her. There was a good breeze blowing and she wondered how the pupils would cope once they got out into the open harbour. Some of them were beginners and shifted about nervously while the boats tacked down the creek.

'Don't worry about them. Dad won't let them drown!'

Becky jumped. Jake had come up behind her, silent on his bare feet. She grinned. 'They don't look very happy.'

Jake stood knee-deep in the water beside

Myrtle and helped Becky hoist the mainsail. 'No,' he said cheerfully. 'We've got some real wallies today.'

He pushed the boat further into the water and then climbed in himself. Becky was at the helm and together they sailed across to the far bank.

'Ready about,' shouted Becky at the last possible moment before they hit the bank. The little boat swung round and they headed back across the water. Jake hardly moved as he pulled in the jib and they zig-zagged expertly down towards the harbour, timing it perfectly so that they never hit the bank but got the maximum wind and the longest runs.

It was a glorious day for a sail, with enough wind to be interesting but not so much that it was frightening. Once they reached the harbour, Becky let Jake have a turn at the helm and he took *Myrtle* as close to the wind as possible, getting from her all the speed she could manage, so that they screamed across the water.

'Let's go and look at the seals,' yelled Jake, and Becky nodded as they changed tack and headed up towards the point.

Before long, they could see a group of black dots in the distance, scattered across the sand and, although Becky had seen them many times before, she still felt a thrill as the dots became larger and could at last be identified as the seal colony basking near the edge of the water.

The seals were never worried by people in boats, but if you tried to land on the point and get out, the whole colony would move, pushing themselves towards the sea and then sliding away out of sight.

Jake sailed the boat in as close as he could, and Becky pulled up the centreboard so that they could get to within a few metres of the shore.

'Look at that one!' said Becky, pointing to a large seal lying on its side scratching its tummy with its flipper. Jake grinned and the seal continued to scratch, staring back at them with dark black eyes set in a solemn whiskery face.

'There's a young one by itself over there,' said Jake, and they both watched as a seal pup, temporarily separated from it's mother, suddenly panicked and galumphed back across the sand to find her.

Becky trailed her hand over the edge of the boat. 'They're all different when you look at them carefully,' she said.

Jake didn't answer, and Becky looked up. He was staring at the sea. 'I saw a really huge one, but its gone under water.'

Becky followed his gaze and, a moment later, a large dark grey head with a Roman nose emerged from the water quite close to the boat.

'There! Look!' said Jake. 'It's much bigger than the others.' It *was* a lot bigger than the others, with a different shaped head and much darker fur.

'That's a grey seal,' said Becky. 'You don't see so many of those.'

Jake frowned. 'I thought they were all the same.'

'No, there are two different kinds here. The Common seal is the one you see all the time. They are the ones on the sand. Then there are the bigger ones – the Grey seals. Some-

times you can see both kinds on the sand, but mostly you see the greys in the water.'

'Oh,' said Jake. 'I didn't realise.'

Becky was puzzled. Jake seemed to know the layout of the harbour, yet nothing about the seals. 'You haven't been sailing here long, then?' asked Becky.

'No. Just this season.'

'Where did you sail before?'

Jake didn't answer and he suddenly seemed

to lose interest in the seals. He looked up at the sky. 'Come on, we ought to get back. I think there's a squall on its way.'

Becky looked at the sky. It didn't look very threatening to her. True, a few clouds were gathering and the wind had strengthened a little, but it was nothing to worry about. 'OK,' she said. 'I'll take the helm.'

Like Jake, Becky sailed as close to the wind as she dared. It was fresher now and whipped up the waves so that, every now and then they were drenched with spray. Becky laughed, exhilarated by her ability to use the wind as she chose. 'Ready about!' she yelled suddenly.

Jake was caught unawares and for the first time their tacking was clumsy and they both had to move fast and put their weight on one side of the boat to avoid capsizing. 'What do you think you're doing?' shouted Jake, angrily. 'We must get back!'

'I just want to show you something,' said Becky. 'It won't take long.'

As she headed the boat towards the opposite shore, Jake tensed, and Becky didn't notice that he gripped the edge of the boat with unnecessary force. 'Where are you going?' he said, harshly.

'It's a secret,' laughed Becky. 'Wait and see.'

'Don't be an idiot, Becky. The weather's turning really bad. We don't want to be caught in a storm. We must get back.'

Suddenly Becky's irritation boiled over. 'Oh shut up, Jake. Don't be such a wimp. I'm not

one of your father's beginners. I've sailed *Myrtle* in much worse weather than this.'

Jake said nothing more, but he looked anxiously over his shoulder as they approached the shore. Then Becky guided the boat round a headland and suddenly they were out of the wind in the shelter of a small humpy island. Running into the island from the sea was a long thin creek and drawn up at the edge of the creek, above the waterline, was the wreck of a house-boat.

'When I was little, my sister and I used to pretend there were pirates living on that wreck,' said Becky.

Jake looked uneasily around him. 'We can't get onto the island, can we?' he said.

Just for a fraction of a second, Becky hesitated. Should she tell Jake what she knew? She had never told anyone else. She decided not to. Emma and she had made it their secret and she would keep it that way.

'No, not really,' she said. 'It's almost impossible to get to now. There are sandbanks all round it and the creek's too narrow to sail up.'

'How did the house-boat get there?'

Becky shrugged. 'I don't know. No-one can remember. They say the sand has shifted over the years and that the creek used to be much wider. You can get to the island by rowing boat, but you have to drop anchor out here at high tide and row in. If you don't get it right you have to drag the boat over the sandbanks.'

'Have you done it?'

'Yes, my sister and I did it once, a few years ago. It was really hard work.'

'Is there anything on the island?'

Becky shook her head. 'Only the birds.'

In silence, they watched black and white oyster-catchers stalking along the muddy creek and common tern on the shingle and out over the water.

'My mum knows all about birds,' said Becky. 'She keeps trying to teach me their names and stuff, but I can never remember.'

Jake shifted impatiently. 'Come on. We ought to go, Becky.'

'No, wait a minute. Just let me listen and see if I can hear any of the bird cries. Then I'll ask Mum what they were.'

Jake drummed his fingers on the edge of the boat, but Becky listened, straining her ears to catch and identify the cries. Suddenly, she stiffened. 'What's that?'

Jake looked up sharply, then he dropped his eyes and held tightly to the jib sheet. 'I didn't hear anything. Come *on*, Becky. My Dad will be needing help and if I'm late back he'll stop me coming out again with you.'

Becky shrugged and took her place at the helm. They were just leaving when Becky heard it again. 'What *is* it? It sounded like someone singing! Do you think there's someone in the wreck?'

'Don't be so stupid,' said Jake sharply. 'You just imagined it.'

'No I *didn't*!'

'Well, I didn't hear anything.'

'It *was* a noise like someone singing,' said Becky firmly.

'It was probably a bird,' said Jake, 'or a seal.'

'Seals don't make any noise,' said Becky.

But soon the strange sound was forgotten. Once they left the shelter of the island, they felt the full force of the squall. They both needed all their concentration to sail the boat back across the harbour and up the home creek to safety.

Chapter Three

That night, Becky told her parents about the noise she'd heard on the island.

'Perhaps it was a seal,' said her mother.

'That's what Jake said, but I told him that seals don't make any noise.'

Mum put down the book she was reading and stretched her arms above her head. 'Well, that's not quite true.'

'But you've always told me that seals are silent.'

'Yes, they **are**, most of the time. But they can make a **kind** of snorting noise if they are cornered and can't get back into the sea.'

'This wasn't a snorting noise,' said Becky. 'It sounded like a person singing.'

Mum took off her specs and started to clean them with a tissue. 'Are you sure it didn't sound like a person *crying*?' she said.

Becky frowned. 'I don't know. I suppose it could have. I only heard it for a moment.'

Carefully, Mum replaced her specs in their case. 'Well, seal pups sometimes make a noise a bit like a baby crying.'

'I never knew that,' said Becky.

'They only do it when they need something. If they are hungry or if they've lost their mother.'

Becky's father broke in. 'I know what you heard,' he said, grinning. 'It was a selchie.'

Mum laughed. 'Oh *yes*, sure to be!' She got to her feet and went into the kitchen to make them all a drink. At the door she turned back. 'Now don't go filling her head with your selchie stories?'

Dad smiled and leant forward. 'Haven't I told you about selchies?' he whispered.

Becky shook her head. 'No. What are they?'

'A selchie is a female seal that has shed its skin and come to live on land as a human.' His voice was so serious that, for a moment, Becky almost believed him. 'Selchies are always beautiful and graceful,' went on Dad, 'and they often fall in love and marry humans. But the call of the sea is very strong and soon they become restless and unhappy on land.'

'So what happens then?' said Becky, wide-eyed.

'Then,' said Dad. 'They search for the skin they shed when they first came on land. If they find it, they can return to the water. But if they can't find it, they pine away and die, longing for the sea.'

'Don't believe a word of it, Becky,' said Mum, coming back into the room.

'Oh, I don't,' laughed Becky.

But the story of the selchie stayed with her and even crept into her dreams that night. It was still with her the next morning and so was the certainty that she *had* heard something, or someone, on the island.

Becky was thoughtful at breakfast and when Mum and Dad suggested a shopping trip to the nearby town, she refused, saying she'd rather go for a walk.

As soon as her parents had gone, Becky studied the chart which was always kept in the cottage, showing the times of the tides. Low tide this morning was ten o'clock. She looked at her watch. It was nine o'clock now. If she left immediately she might just make it.

She got out her bike and rode towards the quay. Here she turned to the right and rode

bumpily along the coastal path for about a mile. Then, hiding her bike behind some bushes, and making sure no-one saw her, she left the path and set off across the marshes.

She hadn't been across this part of the marshes for years. Not since she and Emma had had their great secret. The marshes here were treacherous and no-one tried to walk across them for fear of being sucked down into the mud. But she and Emma had discovered a route over to the island. It was risky — you had to remember exactly the right way — and it took a long time, but it was firm ground all the way.

Becky smiled to herself, remembering that special summer. Day after day, she and Emma had been down here, carefully judging it so that they reached the island at very low tide. No-one ever guessed what they were doing; it was their secret. Becky had been nine that summer, and Emma thirteen.

She set off rather nervously, but she soon found that she hadn't forgotten the way across. She still remembered which creeks were small enough to jump over and where the ground was boggy and treacherous.

She stopped for a moment to catch her breath and as she looked about her she was relieved to see that the marsh was just as bleak and deserted as ever. Although people walked along the coastal path, no-one took much interest in this part of the marshland. All the wildlife — the plants, birds and seals — could be seen much better from the other side of the harbour. On that side there were proper bridges across the creeks and sandy stretches where children could play. Here it was muddy and unfriendly, slippery, treacherous and wild.

She glanced quickly at her watch and then ran on. At last details on the humpy island became clearer and she quickened her pace, slipping and stumbling, determined to get to it before the tide turned.

And then she was there. Standing opposite the island on the very spot where she and Emma had stood when they had first had their idea. Even at low tide, the island was completely surrounded by a wide, deep semi-circular channel, cutting it off from the mainland. And on the side that faced the sea, there were serried ranks of uninviting sand-banks, well above the waterline now that the tide was out.

She had told Jake that the island could only be reached from the sea and then only by rowing a boat at high tide, unless you wanted to drag it across the sand-dunes. But that wasn't quite true.

Becky walked up and down opposite the island, her eyes on the ground, searching for something. At last she found it. Their land-mark, still there, after all this time! There, dug into the marsh, not far from the water's edge, was an upturned brick. Becky dropped to her knees and saw that her initials and Emma's initials, although faded, could still be seen painted on the brick. She smiled, then lay down on her stomach and plunged her arm down into the water.

It was there! After all this time, it was still there! She could feel their causeway, still in place! Becky could hardly believe it. Day after day, she and Emma had dragged stones across the marsh and day after day they had painstakingly sunk layer upon layer onto the mud at the bottom of the channel, building up a causeway of stones. And no-one, except she and Emma, knew of its existence.

Of course, it could only be used for a very short time each day, when the tide was right out. As soon as the tide turned, the water rushed back, spreading quickly over the marshland, hiding treacherous bogs and deep creeks.

Becky looked at her watch again. Ten o'clock exactly. She should be safe for a little while. She stripped down to her bathers and eased herself into the water. Her feet hit the stones sooner than she had expected. Very carefully, she felt her way across the stones at the bottom of the channel. She inched forward, watching all the time in case the water was beginning to rise. Then, at last, she was on the other side. The causeway had done its job. It was still complete.

Becky looked about her wondering if she had, after all, imagined the sound of singing. She walked round the tiny island, looking for signs of a stranded seal pup. But all she found were startled sea-birds. She glanced up the

creek which ran out to sea, then looked at her watch again. She couldn't spend long here, otherwise she would be cut off by the tide. She would take a quick look at the wreck, just for old times sake, then she must hurry back.

It was not much changed, still lying there on its side, battered by wind and rain, paint peeled off long ago. A sad, drunken old house-boat. Becky walked round it uneasily. It still held some mystery for her. It always had, ever since she and Emma pretended that pirates lived in it.

Last time she'd been here, Emma had had to lift her up to see through the porthole into the cabin. Now, she was tall enough to see in for herself. She frowned. She knew something was different, but at first she didn't realise what. Then she saw the glass in the porthole. It was new glass. Last time, there had been no glass at all.

Becky flattened herself against the side of the boat, hardly daring to breathe. If there was new glass in the porthole, someone had put it there, and put it there for a reason. And that someone might be around, might even be inside the house-boat now! With a thumping heart, she edged nearer the porthole and forced herself to take a quick look inside.

The next moment she was running from the wreck, stumbling, splashing across the causeway, then, pausing only to snatch her clothes from the ground, she raced back over the marshes as the incoming tide spread its fingers behind her.

Chapter Four

When at last she reached the place where she had hidden her bike, Becky flung herself down on the ground, gasping for breath, and tried to think calmly.

Someone had been living on the house-boat! Inside, it had been cleaned and repaired. There was some food, a cooker, and even clean blankets spread over a bunk. But there was something else. Something that was much more frightening than the glass at the porthole or the blankets or the food or the cooker. Something that had made her eyes widen and the hairs on her neck stand up and lent wings to her feet as she raced back across the marsh.

It had been on the floor. A grey motionless shape. At first, she hadn't realised what it was. Then, when she looked more closely she recognised it. It was a sealskin!

If this had happened anywhere else, Becky would have shrugged it off, found some explanation. But there, on that barren island, things were different. The island had taken hold of her imagination and its mysterious atmosphere was creeping over her just as it had before, when they'd built the causeway.

'It can't be true!' Becky muttered to herself. 'It *can't* be!' But the longer she thought about it, the more the idea took hold. After all, why would any human choose to live on that wreck on a bare island with nothing but birds for company?

She had no idea how long she lay there, her thoughts in a frightened jumble, but at last she got to her feet and pushed her bike slowly back along the coastal path to the quay. And as she pedalled slowly up the hill back to the cottage, one word kept repeating itself in her mind.

'Selchie!'

She had been so absorbed in her own thoughts that she had forgotten everything else. Forgotten it was Saturday and that Emma was coming up from London for the weekend. She got quite a shock when she saw another car parked outside the gate. Emma had seen her

coming and she ran out to the road as Becky
dismounted from her bike.

'We thought you were never coming!' she
laughed, hugging her. 'Where have you been
all morning?'

Becky smiled. 'Oh, just down to the marshes.'

'What, *our* marshes?'

'Yes.'

'Tell me all about it after lunch,' said Emma,
and she put her arm round Becky's shoulders
and propelled her towards the door.

All through lunch they chatted and laughed. Emma was full of stories about her job, her flat and her friends. Later in the afternoon, the whole family went for a walk along the coastal path. Emma and Becky walked in front.

'How far did you go this morning?' asked Emma.

Becky pointed. 'Right over there.'

'What! Right to the island?'

Becky nodded.

'That was brave. Did you remember the way and where all the bogs are and the wide creeks and everything?'

'Yes. It all came back to me even though I'd not been there for years. Not since…you know.'

'Since the causeway?'

Becky nodded.

Emma ran her hand through her hair and then stretched. 'Did you ever tell anyone else about the causeway?'

Becky shook her head. 'No.'

'Nor me,' said Emma. 'What a summer that was. We worked and worked at it didn't we?' she laughed. 'I expect it got washed away the next winter!'

'No, Em, it didn't,' said Becky quickly. Then she wished she'd kept quiet.

Emma stopped in her tracks. 'It's not still there?'

Becky nodded.

'You mean you went right over to the island today at low tide, using our causeway?'

'Umm.' Becky nodded again.

'That's incredible. I must go and have a look myself. We'll go over together tomorrow.'

Becky said nothing. She almost told Emma what she'd seen, but then she decided, after all, to keep it to herself. Emma was grown-up now. She wouldn't find the island mysterious any more. She wouldn't be affected by its magic. And she certainly wouldn't believe in a selchie woman. Quickly she changed the subject.

'There's a new family here this year. They're called the Fieldings and they run a sailing school.'

'That's good,' said Emma. 'There hasn't been anyone teaching sailing here for years. Are the children nice? How old are they?'

'Yes. They seem OK. Jake's fourteen and

Penny's about your age, I think.'

Emma bent down to pick a piece of grass. She chewed at it thoughtfully. 'Penny Fielding,' she said slowly. 'I was at school with a girl called Penny Fielding. I wonder if it's the same one?'

'She's quite small, with long black hair.'

'Sounds like her. I'd like to see her again. Do you know where they live?'

Becky shook her head. 'No, but I should think they'll be down at the quay now. It's almost sailing time.'

Emma looked at her watch. 'Yes, you're right. I tell you what. We'll go back there in a minute, then I can say hello to Penny before we take old *Myrtle* out.'

Becky smiled. 'OK.'

A little later, they made their way back to the quay. They could see all the Fieldings getting the boats ready to go out. Emma and Becky walked over to them.

'Penny!' shouted Emma.

Penny Fielding stopped what she was doing and raised her head. She was too far away for Emma and Becky to see the startled look on her face as she recognised Emma, or hear her urgent whisper to Mrs Fielding who was working beside her.

Emma came nearer and stood by the boat. 'Hi Penny!'

Penny Fielding turned to look at her. 'Oh. Hi Emma.'

'Hello Mrs Fielding!'

Mrs Fielding had her back to Emma and she didn't turn round, but kept on working. 'Hello Emma,' she said.

Then Becky saw Jake and went over to talk to him. 'My sister's here for the weekend, Jake, so I'll sail with her. But she goes back to London on Sunday night, so could you come out on Monday?'

Jake was watching Penny and Emma and he wasn't really listening. 'Sure', he said, without turning his head.

Becky went to get *Myrtle* ready and, after a while, Emma joined her, looking puzzled.

'What's the matter?' said Becky.

'What? Oh, it's nothing really. Just that Penny didn't seem very pleased to see me. And her mother...her mother was...I don't know... different, somehow. Oh, never mind. Come on, let's get old *Myrtle* out into the water!'

Sailing was second nature to Emma and she didn't need to think what to do. It was just as well, because her thoughts were elsewhere. She hardly spoke to Becky, and when they came in, she helped to make the boat safe and then disappeared, saying she'd meet Becky back at the cottage.

Becky put on the cover and watched her sister run to the other side of the quay. Then she saw Penny Fielding some distance ahead of Emma. Penny looked over her shoulder and started to run. But Emma ran too and caught up with her. She grabbed her arm, forcing her to stop. Then they walked on together, out of Becky's sight.

That evening, when Becky asked Emma about Penny Fielding, she said. 'Oh, we were just chatting about old school friends.'

The next morning, Emma had forgotten all about the causeway and the island. She was unlike herself, quiet and moody, and after lunch she said she had to get back to London early. Becky waved until her car turned the corner, hurt at Emma's sudden change of mood and convinced it had something to do with Penny Fielding.

Chapter Five

That evening, Becky took *Myrtle* out by herself.
The Fielding boats had already left and Jake
was nowhere to be seen. Becky was relieved
because she wanted to be alone.

She approached the island and sailed as
near as she could, but there was no sign of life
on the house-boat. Becky waited and listened,
but she heard no singing. All she heard were
the birds and the wind and the sea.

That night she dreamt again about the selchie
woman and the next morning she woke up
restless and irritable. She longed to tell
someone about what she had seen on the
island, but that would give away the secret of
the causeway and if a selchie woman did live on
the house-boat, she shouldn't be disturbed.

When it was time to sail the next evening,
Becky couldn't find Jake, and she was just
about to go out on her own again, when she

caught sight of him talking to his father. She waved and Jake came over. 'Do you want to come?' she asked.

Jake shrugged his shoulders. 'Yeah, OK.'

'You sure? You don't sound very keen,' said Becky, stung by his attitude.

'Umm. Sorry, there've been a lot of things going on, that's all.'

'What sort of things?'

'Oh, just this and that,' said Jake, vaguely. Then he got in the boat and they set off. Jake asked if he could take the helm and this time Becky didn't argue. He seemed edgy and distracted and she noticed that he kept well away from the island. It was a peaceful sail and the sea was calm in the fading light.

'This will be the last evening sail for a while,' said Becky.

Jake nodded. 'We'll only be doing morning lessons tomorrow.'

They sailed on in silence, but it was an awkward silence, with neither of them relaxed.

'Did you know your sister was at school with my sister?' asked Becky, trying to ease the tension.

'Umm,' Jake grunted.

'Funny, that, wasn't it?' said Becky.

'Hysterical,' said Jake and swung the boat round without warning, taking Becky by surprise. Instinctively she put her weight in the right place and pulled the jib across, but she was furious.

'Why did you do that?'

'You should have realised. You weren't paying attention.'

'You didn't *say* anything,' shouted Becky, her eyes blazing. 'How could I know if you didn't say anything!'

Jake didn't answer and in stony silence they sailed back up the creek while behind them the sunset streaked pink and gold across the sky.

It was deep twilight by the time Becky rode home, and, as she wobbled up the hill, the beam of her bike lamp picked out several startled rabbits still grazing on the verge. Halfway up the hill, she stopped and got off, too tired to pedal any further. She held her wrist in front of the lamp to see the time. 'Oh *no*!' she said out loud, as she stared at the space where her watch should have been. She'd taken it off just before they went sailing and had forgotten to put it on again.

Wearily, she mounted her bike again and rode back down the hill. The quay was deserted and it was getting quite dark. Becky propped up her bike near to where *Myrtle* was moored. Then she crouched down and swept the beam of light over the ground.

Yes! There it was, just as she had left it. Smiling with relief, she strapped it on and was just about to stand up and walk back to her bike when she heard a sound in the distance. It was the unmistakable chug-chug noise of an engine. Becky frowned. Who on earth could be coming down the creek in a motor-boat now, in semi-darkness? Still squatting on the ground, she snapped off the torch and waited nervously as the noise came closer.

She saw lights on the motor-boat as it edged its way closer. They were very dim lights. Whoever was in the boat must know the creek well. She shivered and watched as the motor-boat passed her and chug-chugged very slowly round the bend until it stopped by the Fieldings mooring.

The bend in the creek hid the boat from her view. Hardly knowing why, Becky crept back along the bank until she was right beside the Fielding's boats. She crouched down, out of sight and watched. In the dim lights she could just see the outline of someone tying the motor-boat to one of the other dinghies and then putting a cover over the outboard motor.

Suddenly the lights went out and she could see nothing at all. But a moment later, a torch was snapped on and the figure in the motor-boat climbed quietly over the other boats and then jumped down on to the bank. As he jumped, the torch jerked upwards and Becky caught a glimpse of his face. It was Jake!

Becky laughed with relief and stood up. 'Jake!' she shouted. She was quite unprepared for what happened next.

Jake swung round and for a dreadful moment she thought he was going to hit her. Instead, he grabbed her by the shoulders and started to shake her. 'What the hell are you doing, spying on me like that?'

She had never seen him like this before. He was stuttering with fury. 'Let me go!' she shouted. 'Stop shaking me.'

'What were you doing here?' he repeated.

Becky swallowed. She was determined not to cry. 'I left my watch behind. I came back to fetch it.'

Jake relaxed his grip then, but his voice was still harsh. 'Just keep out of my way in future. Do you hear?'

Becky wriggled herself free and stood facing him in the darkness. 'What's the matter with you Jake! What's happened?' Then, when he didn't answer, she went on. 'It's the island, isn't it? It's got something to do with the island.'

'What?'

'You know about the house-boat, don't you? About the selchie on the house-boat?'

Jake gave an involuntary gasp, but in a

second he had recovered himself, and when he spoke again, his voice was calm. 'What do you mean, Becky,' he said slowly. 'Tell me what you mean?'

'I've seen inside the house-boat,' she said. 'I've seen the mended porthole, and the stove and the blankets and the...' She couldn't bring herself to mention the sealskin.

In the dark, Jake frowned and gripped his torch. 'But *how*?' he said, almost to himself. 'I know no-one else has been across the dunes from the sea. We've been watching. *How* have you seen?'

'There's another way,' said Becky. 'You can get to the island by land.'

'No you can't. It's not possible. We've checked!'

'No-one else knows about it. No-one except me and Emma.'

'*What*! Are you sure?'

'Of course I'm sure. How do you think I got onto the island?'

'Have you told anyone else about this, about what you saw on the island? Have you told your parents or Emma?'

'No. I thought they'd laugh at me. They wouldn't believe in the selchie.'

'The selchie?' Jake repeated. He was about to say something else, but he stopped.

'I'd better go,' said Becky. 'Mum and Dad will be getting worried.'

She started to walk away, but Jake called after her. 'Becky!'

'Yes.'

'Will you promise me something? It's very important.'

Becky stood still. 'What is it?'

'Will you promise not to say anything to anyone about the...er...selchie.'

'Don't worry, I won't. I think she should be left on her own, poor thing. Anyway, I don't want people thinking I'm daft.'

'I don't think you're daft. I believe you.'

There was a brief silence, then Jake went on. 'And don't say anything to your parents about what happened just now. I didn't mean to frighten you. I was scared too.'

'OK then,' mumbled Becky, after a moment's hesitation. 'But you must promise not to tell anyone else about the way across to the island from the marsh.'

'I promise,' said Jake, but he looked away
from her as he spoke.

Chapter Six

Becky's parents were cross when she came back late. 'What have you been doing? It's very late. You can't have been sailing in the dark!'

Wearily, Becky explained. 'I'm sorry. We set off late, then we got talking and then I lost my watch and had to go back for it...' She said nothing about the island or the selchie woman or about Jake's trip in the motorboat. And she certainly didn't mention how frightened she'd been when he shook her.

'All right, love,' said Mum, with an impatient sigh. 'But don't be so late again. I know you and Jake are both good sailors, but even so, Dad and I were beginning to get very worried.'

'Sorry,' said Becky.

As Becky went up the stairs, she heard her mother say, 'From tomorrow they won't be able to sail in the evenings. The tide's not high until after dark.'

Becky ran a hot bath and then lowered

herself into it, sinking down and letting the warm water relax her aching limbs. And as she lay there she went over the events of the last few days in her mind.

Did *all* the Fielding family know about the selchie woman? she wondered. Was that why Jim Fielding had warned Jake to be careful when Dad had first suggested a sail in *Myrtle*? Were the whole family protecting the selchie from the outside world? That would certainly explain why Jake got so uptight when she had shown him the island on their first sail together. And it might explain where he'd been tonight in the motorboat. Perhaps he'd been over to the island in near darkness at high-tide to visit the selchie.

But no, it wasn't just that. There were other things that didn't fit, other things that couldn't be explained. Her thoughts kept returning to her sister, Emma. On the Saturday morning, Emma had been her usual cheerful self, just the same as always. Then she had seen Penny Fielding. Penny hadn't been pleased to see Emma. Why not? Emma had said they'd been pretty good friends at school. And Emma had also said that Mrs Fielding was 'different' somehow. What did she mean by different?

And there was the time when Becky had seen Emma run after Penny and grab her arm, forcing her to stop and talk. What had they really been talking about then? And why was Emma so quiet and thoughtful afterwards? Emma was normally open and straightforward, but she had clammed up when Becky asked her about her conversation with Penny. Emma was hiding something, Becky was sure of it. Emma knew something about the Fieldings that no-one else knew.

As she soaked in the bath, all this kept churning round in her head. The sound of the telephone penetrated her thoughts and lazily she got out of the bath and started to dry herself. She heard voices. First her mother's, then her father's. Something in their tone made her stop and listen. Her mother's voice was shrill, questioning, and her father's had the sharp edge of anxiety. The telephone was put down but the voices went on. Her father and mother were talking urgently together. Something was wrong.

Quickly, Becky finished drying herself and wrapped her dressing-gown round her. She hurried down the stairs and opened the door into the living room. Her parents were standing close together and they turned towards her as she came in. Becky looked from one to the other. Mum had been crying and her face was streaked with tears, and Dad looked white and strained.

'What's the matter? What's happened? Who were you talking to? Why are you looking like that?'

Dad cleared his throat. Gently he released Mum and came over to Becky. 'Don't worry, love. It's probably nothing. I'm sure there's a simple explanation.'

'What do you mean?'

'That was Emma's flatmate on the telephone,' said Dad. 'She was ringing to see if Emma was better.'

'Better?' said Becky. 'But she wasn't ill, was she?'

Mum swallowed and said quietly. 'Apparently Emma telephoned the flat yesterday to say that she wasn't well so she was going to stay on here for a couple of days until she got better.'

'Here?'

'Yes. She said she'd be here at the cottage.'

'But she left yesterday!'

Dad nodded and there was silence for a moment while Becky tried to take it in. It wasn't like Emma to deceive her parents. Something must be wrong.

'I think I should telephone the police,' said

Dad.

'Oh no! Surely that's not necessary!' said Mum.

Dad looked wretched. 'Well, I don't want to do it, but just in case...' He didn't finish the sentence.

Becky stood there, in her dressing gown, too

horrified to speak. Something must have happened to Emma. Someone must have got her, be holding her against her will. She wouldn't do this to Mum and Dad. Not Emma. Then, unbidden, an image flashed across her mind. Once more, she saw Emma running after Penny Fielding…

'Dad!' said Becky.

Her father was holding the telephone, about to dial the police. He stopped and looked at her face. Something he saw there made him put down the telephone. 'What is it Becky! Do you know something?'

'Not exactly,' she said, biting her lip, 'but…' Becky hesitated. 'Well, it's just something I saw.'

'What? When?'

'It was on Saturday, after we'd been sailing. Emma saw Penny Fielding in the distance and went running after her. Then, when Penny saw Emma she started to run away. But Emma caught her up and grabbed her arm.'

'Is that all?' said Dad.

Becky nodded.

'But on Saturday evening Emma was very

quiet, wasn't she,' said Mum thoughtfully. 'I wonder…'

'There was another thing,' said Becky. 'It wasn't just Penny. Emma said Mrs Fielding was different and didn't seem to want to see her either.'

'Different? In what way different?'

Becky shrugged. 'I don't know. She wouldn't tell me any more about it after she'd been talking to Penny.'

'So you think Penny Fielding may know where Emma is now?' said Dad.

'I don't *know*,' said Becky, and her voice trembled. She suddenly felt very tired and shaky. First, she had been really scared and upset by Jake, and now Emma had gone missing. She couldn't bear to think of anyone hurting Emma.

'Do you know where the Fieldings live?' asked Dad.

Becky shook her head, not trusting her voice.

'Never mind. We can find out easily enough.' He turned back to the telephone and made a couple of calls, then he picked up his car keys and headed for the door.

'You're not going on your own,' said Mum, firmly. 'I'm coming with you.'

'So am I,' said Becky.

'Why don't you go to bed, love,' said Mum. 'There's nothing you can do. We won't be long, I promise.'

'No!' Although she was close to tears she almost shouted her reply.

Mum sighed. 'All right. Run and put some clothes on. We'll wait for you in the car.'

Becky raced up the stairs, flung on some clean jeans and a jersey, and within minutes was in the back seat of the car, lacing up her trainers.

It took them a while to find the cottage. It was tucked away in a courtyard off the main street of the town. Dad just managed to squeeze the car into the courtyard. He got out quickly, rammed the car keys into his trouser pocket and strode over to the door. There was no bell or knocker so he banged on the door with his fist. Mum and Becky followed him and they stood together, huddled in the deep shadows. There was no sign of life from the cottage.

'Perhaps they've all gone to bed,' said Mum.

'Then they'll just have to get *out* of bed,' said Dad grimly, and banged on the door again.

At last a light went on and they heard footsteps coming down the passage. A bolt was drawn back and the door opened. Jim Fielding stood in the doorway. He had a jacket slung over his pyjamas and he didn't look at all pleased to see them.

Chapter Seven

Jim Fielding stared at them and, for a moment, no-one said anything. Then Dad blurted out, 'Is Penny there?'

Jim frowned. 'Why do you want her. She's asleep.'

Dad was about to say something else when Mum interrupted him. 'Our daughter, Emma, is missing, Mr Fielding. We think Penny might be able to help us find her.'

Becky was watching Jim Fielding's face. The light was behind him and she couldn't see the expression in his eyes, but she saw his jaw tighten. The moments ticked by and Jim Fielding said nothing. Then he seemed to come to a decision.

'You'd better come in,' he said gruffly, and moved aside to let them pass down the passage. They shuffled past him into the kitchen. Becky blinked in the brightness and looked about the room. It was clean but sparsely furnished.

It didn't feel like a home and she guessed it was rented for the season. Jim Fielding followed them in.

'I'm sorry to trouble you,' said Mum, 'but we're terribly worried. Can we seen Penny now?'

Once again, Jim Fielding hesitated. Mum frowned. 'Is your wife here?'

'No,' he said, abruptly, then turned back and walked down the passage and up the stairs. Becky and her parents looked at each other, their faces strained. Mum pulled back a chair and sat at the kitchen table. 'I hope Penny can help. I can't bear to think of Emma...'

'Don't!' said Dad, sharply. He went to stand behind Mum and put his hands on her shoulders. 'Don't start imagining things. There's probably a perfectly simple explanation.' But he didn't look convinced.

At last there were footsteps on the stairs and Mr Fielding, Penny and Jake came into the kitchen. Penny came in first and met Mum's eyes. She immediately looked away.

Mum stood up and gripped the edge of the table. 'Penny. Do you know where Emma is?

Have you any idea what's happened to her?'

'No,' said Penny quickly. 'Why should I?' But she didn't look at Mum when she spoke. She fiddled with her dressing gown and stared across at the sink.

Becky broke in. 'But it was after she'd seen you that she went all funny. I saw her chase after you and you tried to run away. Why did you try and run away, Penny?'

Penny didn't answer.

Becky was near to tears. 'Somebody must know *something*,' she shouted. She turned to Jake. 'What about you, Jake? Do you know what's happened to Emma.'

Jake shook his head, but he looked uncomfortable.

Dad turned to Jim Fielding and sighed. 'I'm sorry we've disturbed you all. We thought there was just a chance that Penny might be able to help. I'll go to the police now. I don't think there's anything else we can do.'

Penny's head shot up and she moved nearer to her father. 'Dad,' she whispered. 'We can't let them go to the police. Someone will see them. All sorts of rumours will start flying about. It will spoil everything!'

'Be quiet, Penny!' Jim Fielding's voice was furious, but Penny wouldn't be quiet. She shook his arm.

'Don't you see, Dad. We've *got* to tell them! It's the only way. Otherwise the whole thing will be ruined.'

Jim Fielding stared at Penny and his voice was hoarse when he replied. 'We *can't*! I promised.'

'But that was before Emma came,' said Penny gently. 'We weren't to know she'd be here. It was a chance in a million!'

Jim Fielding continued to look at Penny, searching her face. Then he sat down in a chair and put his head in his hands.

Penny walked across the room and stood in front of Mum. This time she looked her straight in the face. 'It's all right,' said Penny. 'Emma's quite safe. She's with the police.'

'With the police! Why? What's happened. I don't understand!'

Penny took a deep breath. She looked across at her father but his head was still in his hands. 'Dad?' said Penny. Jim Fielding looked up.

'Dad. *Please* tell them.'

His eyes were red and his voice was hardly more than a whisper. 'All right,' he said at last. 'This is very difficult for me,' he began, then he stopped and swallowed. Becky couldn't believe it. He was near to tears, struggling not to break down. 'I…well, I can't…'

'Shall I tell them, Dad?' said Penny.

Jim Fielding nodded.

Penny was standing directly under the light. Small and poised, with her gleaming black hair, she suddenly seemed much older than her years. 'It all started about two years ago,' said Penny, quietly. 'When I was still at school.'

'With Emma,' put in Becky.

'Yes, with Emma. In fact, when it all started, Emma was the only person I told.' She smiled briefly. 'The only person outside the family who knew how worried we were. I was desperate to talk to someone about it. Someone I could trust.'

'And then Emma turned up here!' muttered Jake.

Mum frowned. 'But what did Emma know? I don't understand.'

Penny sighed. 'It was Mum. She'd always been the kind of person who really cared about people – she'd do anything for anyone. Then, a couple of years ago she started to change. It was very gradual and at first it was only little things. She'd promise to do something, then forget to do it. Or she'd say she was coming to the school for a play or a concert and she wouldn't turn up.

'Then later she started lying to us about where she was going. She became very secretive and she stopped caring about herself, about the way she looked. And in the end she didn't even seem to care about us. Dad and Mum started to have rows all the time. Mostly about money. Mum was spending a lot of money and there was nothing to show for it. Although she was spending much less on food and things for the house the money was going somewhere, and she wouldn't tell Dad where.'

Mr Fielding cut in. 'She was very clever, you see,' he said. 'She only used cheques to pay the supermarket or for the children's school clothes. Bills that I would never question. But for everything else she used cash, so I could 'never find out what she spent it on.'

'She had her own money, too,' said Jake, speaking for the first time. 'She's a nurse and she worked at the local hospital.'

'Yes,' said Jim Fielding. 'She'd been back at work for some years.'

'Anyway,' said Penny. 'Just when things were really bad, she stopped spending money – at least we thought she'd stopped – and for a while everything was better. But then something happened and we found out the truth. At last we realised what she had been doing.'

They were all looking at Penny and suddenly her face crumpled. The tears welled up in her eyes and she clenched and unclenched her hand. Jim Fielding went over to her and held her tightly against him. Over her head, he addressed Becky and her parents.

'You've probably already guessed what was wrong with my wife,' he said.

There was silence in the room, then Mum said what they'd all been thinking. 'Was she on drugs?' Her voice was low and full of compassion.

'Yes,' said Jim Fielding. 'My wife had become a drug addict.'

Chapter Eight

Penny was still crying and Jake looked desperately unhappy.

'Jake,' said Mum. 'Why don't you put the kettle on. I think we could all do with a hot drink.'

Glad of something to do, Jake went over to the sink and filled the electric kettle.

'It must be dreadful for you all,' said Mum softly. 'I'm so sorry. If there's anything we can do to help…'

'But you still haven't said why Emma's with the police!' blurted out Becky.

Penny broke away from her father's arms and wiped her eyes and blew her nose. 'It's for her own protection,' she said. 'You see, she knew Mum when she was well and then she watched her change gradually, but there are some things that don't change – mannerisms, expressions, things like that.'

'I don't understand, Penny,' said Dad. 'What

are you trying to tell us?'

'What she is trying to tell you,' said Jim
Fielding, 'is that the woman with us, posing as
my wife, is not my wife, but my wife's twin
sister.'

'Her identical twin,' said Penny.

'And Emma realised!' said Becky.

'Emma realised that although she looks just
like Mum, she isn't Mum. And *no-one* must
know that,' said Penny. 'No-one except a few
policemen and ourselves. Especially not now.
So we told the police what had happened –
that Emma had seen my aunt and knew it
wasn't Mum, and they thought it would be
better to keep Emma out of the way, just until
the end of this week in case anyone saw us
talking together and tried to question her. She
knows all about it now and she's agreed to stay
in hiding.'

'But *why?*' said Becky. 'What's the point...'

Jim Fielding was helping Jake make mugs of
coffee. As he handed them round, he said,
'Did anyone see you come here tonight?'

Dad shook his head. 'I don't think so.'

'I hope not, for your sake,' said Jim

Fielding, grimly. 'We've not encouraged
people to come here to the house. We see
people all the time down at the sailing school
of course, but not here. If there is even the
slightest suspicion that other people are
involved, then everything we've been doing
for the past few months will be wasted.'

Dad frowned as he sipped his coffee. 'Could
you explain,' he asked. 'We still don't
understand...'

'Yes,' said Jim slowly. 'Yes, I think we owe that

to you.' Then he went on. 'I never suspected my wife was on drugs. I suppose it was stupid of me, but it never even crossed my mind. She'd been ill and rather depressed and it may have started after that. Perhaps she managed to get something from the hospital, I really don't know. But by the time we did discover, she was hooked and she had no hope of breaking the habit on her own.'

'How did you discover?' asked Mum, gently.

'My sister-in-law, who was living abroad at the time, came over for a visit. As soon as she saw my wife, she realised what none of *us* had realised. She saw how much she'd changed and she immediately suspected drugs. But, much worse than that, she also realised where the extra money was coming from.'

'Had she been selling drugs, too?' asked Mum.

'Yes.' Jim Fielding looked round at them all and there were tears in his eyes. 'It was horrible, but it's not an unusual story. She needed more supplies; she couldn't pay for them. Somehow she was persuaded to sell the stuff herself so she got a cut of the money.'

'Did she tell you all this?'

'Yes. My sister-in-law confronted her and I think it was a relief to confess. We tried to persuade her to get help and she agreed, but then the blackmail started.'

'Blackmail!' said Dad. 'But who...how?'

'That's the trouble with these people. The threats never came direct. They were passed on through a chain of people. But I never doubted they were serious.'

'What sort of threats?'

'Oh, they were going to expose her, disgrace her family, make life unbearable for her if she stopped pushing drugs for them. I'm a teacher. I love my job and she couldn't bear to think I might lose it or that Penny and Jake would suffer because of her. She was ill and terrified.'

'So what happened then?'

'Well, then my sister-in-law did an incredibly brave thing. She offered to take my wife's place.'

'How? What do you mean?'

'She told the police what had been going on and they referred her to the drugs squad. Together, with the police, we worked out a plan of action to try and find out where the drugs were coming from and who was the organiser. My wife left her job and told her contact with the drug supplier that she wanted to get more involved, and that I did, too. It took a long time to persuade them that the whole family went along with the drug-pushing, but in the end they came to believe that we were as greedy for money as they were. Then, every now and then, my sister-in-law would replace my wife until, eventually, it was always her, and not my wife, who met the contacts.'

Jim Fielding took a gulp of coffee and continued. 'We had to be very careful that they were never seen together but it wasn't as hard as you might think. By this time my wife had cut herself off from nearly all her friends so she was seeing very few people. And, once my sister-in-law had taken her place, we got my wife away to a clinic in another part of the country.'

'Is she getting any better?' asked Mum.

'It's terribly slow, but she is making progress. She's really trying, for all our sakes.'

'But what's going on here, now?' asked

Becky. 'Why is there someone in the house-boat on the island? Why...'

'What are you talking about, Becky?' said Mum.

Jim Fielding held up his hand. 'Yes. I'm coming to that. It's a long story, but my sister-in-law has become trusted by the organisers of the drug ring. They were looking for a new place to bring drugs into the country and they chose the island as an ideal spot. She offered to be their contact here, at least during the summer months. I've sailed all my life, and so have the rest of the family, so we set up the sailing school as a cover.'

'And have they brought any drugs in yet?' asked Dad.

'No, not yet. But one night this week, on the high tide, they will do their first drop.'

'So your sister-in-law is out there, now?'

Jim nodded. 'Yes, and she'll be there every night until they come.'

'And what about the police?'

'They know, of course. And there are plain clothes drug squad detectives everywhere. You see, it's really important we catch these people this time, because, as it's the first time in a new place, two of the main organisers will be coming over to see that everything goes smoothly.'

'How will they come?'

'They'll come by boat and do the drop one night this week, but we don't know which night. They may even be in the harbour now. They'll be watching every movement near the island to make sure that no-one goes near it except us.'

'So you won't be able to get any police on the island?'

Jim shook his head. 'These people are criminals. There's a lot at stake and they've been very careful. Even though I'm sure they don't suspect us, they only told us two days ago that this would be the week and they made it clear that they already had the island under observation. The island is a long way from any moorings, so any boat out there at night would raise their suspicions.'

'Couldn't you get people over to the island in your motor-boat?' asked Dad. 'Surely someone could lie hidden in the bottom of the boat...'

Jim Fielding shook his head. 'It's just not worth the risk. We don't know who is watching us or when or where. So far they trust us and we've got to keep their trust until they make the drop.'

'What about the police?' said Dad. 'What are they doing?'

'They are all standing by. The police launch will try and intercept any small boat making for the island across the dunes at high tide. But it will be terribly difficult at night and it does put my sister-in-law in a very dangerous position.' Jim Fielding sighed.

'What a pity the island can't be reached by land,' said Mum.

'Then they wouldn't have chosen it!'

Becky looked up sharply and her eyes met Jake's. 'Did you tell them?' she asked. 'Did you tell them about the marsh?'

Jake cleared his throat. 'Yes…I'm sorry, Becky. I did mention it to Dad, but he said we couldn't involve you. It was far too risky.'

'Well, you can now, can't you, Mr Fielding? No-one else knows about it, only Emma and me. Not even the locals know!'

'What *are* you talking about Becky?' said Mum.

All the fear, excitement and fatigue of the evening suddenly hit Becky and she started to tremble. 'There *is* a way over to the island by land, Mum. It's very complicated and if you get it wrong you can get sucked down into the marsh. But I know it. Emma and I discovered it five years ago. I can lead you over the marsh at low tide and I can take you over the channel, too.'

'What!' said Dad. 'You never told us. Are you sure?'

Becky nodded. 'Certain. I've been there already this holidays. When Jake and I went for our first sail together I thought I heard someone singing on the island, so the next day I went over by land to check, and that was when I saw inside the house-boat and realised someone had been using it.'

'But why didn't you tell us?'

Becky shrugged. 'I knew you'd be worried if you thought I'd been across. And anyway, it's always been a secret between me and Emma.'

'But the whole of that marsh is treacherous,' said Dad. 'And the channel round the island is wide and deep.'

'Emma and I made a causeway,' said Becky. 'And it's still there.'

Jim Fielding stared at Becky. Very slowly he passed his hand over his brow. Then he spoke. 'It might be the answer,' he said, softly. 'We know they won't move if there are any other boats out there. We've been puzzling all week how we can catch them red-handed, actually delivering the stuff onto the island. If we don't do that, we can prove nothing.' He turned to Mum and Dad. 'Would you let Becky help us?'

Mum and Dad looked at each other. 'I don't see how we can refuse,' said Mum.

Becky sat very still. It wasn't the journey across the marsh that frightened her, nor the walk through the channel across the causeway. It was the image that suddenly came into her head. The image of the discarded sealskin lying on the floor of the house-boat. Was Jake's aunt the person she'd heard singing? Or had it been another voice? The voice of a selchie?

Chapter Nine

Jim Fielding smiled at Becky. It was the first time she'd ever seen him smile. 'Will you help us, Becky?'

She nodded. 'I'll try.'

'Good girl!' Then he became brisk and efficient. Maps were brought out, more coffee was drunk, and, before long, a plan had been made.

It was very late when Becky and her parents crept away, leaving the cottage as quietly as they could. At the door, Jim Fielding whispered, 'Good luck tomorrow, Becky. We're relying on you. I'll make all the necessary contacts but you won't hear from us again unless the dealers make the drop tonight. If they do, then we'll have to go ahead with the plans we've made already. But if we *can* get people onto the island before they arrive, then we stand a much better chance of catching them.'

Becky hardly slept for the rest of the night and when she got up she was tired, stiff and anxious. As the day dragged by, they all waited, uneasily. Her parents were unnaturally bright and cheerful and Becky knew they were trying to help her relax. But she was too worried to relax. She kept seeing the treacherous marsh. What if the police were late and they missed the tide? What if she forgot her way this time? What if the drug dealers followed her? What if..?

She was relieved when, at last, it was time to go. Becky was dressed in shorts and a t-shirt and round her waist she had tied her blue and white striped jersey. This was how they would recognise her. The plain clothes police would be looking for a girl with a blue and white jersey tied round her waist.

They all drove down to the quay together and then got out of the car and set off along the coastal path. They walked in silence, and as they walked they glanced furtively about them. Was this man coming towards them a detective? Or that one, over there, wearing a blue anorak? But nothing seemed unusual. It was a perfectly normal summer's day, with several walkers enjoying the sights and sounds of the coast.

'I wish something would happen,' whispered Becky. 'I'm scared.'

Dad squeezed her hand. 'Try and be brave,' he said.

Mum said nothing.

A little further on, Becky stopped. 'This is the place,' she said.

'Perhaps we should stay with you?' suggested Mum.

Dad hesitated, but then he said 'No. I don't think we should. They probably won't approach her until she's on her own. Just in case...'

Mum hugged her. 'Take care,' she whispered, and then her parents were gone, walking on down the path, hand in hand. Becky longed for them to look back and wave, but they didn't. Becky knew why. Jim Fielding had warned them: 'Whatever you do, don't draw attention to her.'

Becky slid down the bank until she was at the edge of the marsh, just where she had sat a few days ago, frightened and breathless after seeing inside the house-boat. She was frightened again as she looked across the marsh. Her hands were clammy and she tensed at each footfall which passed by on the path behind her. If the police didn't come soon, it would be too late.

'Becky?'

Becky slewed round and fell back awkwardly as she tried to get to her feet and look at the man standing behind her. She hadn't even heard him coming!

He was quite young and he didn't look much like a policeman. He was wearing shorts and strong hiking shoes and on his back was a bulging rucksack. He spoke again and his voice was very quiet. 'Are you Becky?'

Becky nodded. The man took his rucksack off his back and sat down. He smiled at her. 'Don't look so scared. It's all right. Jim Fielding sent me.'

'Are you alone?' whispered Becky, still shaking. 'I thought there'd be more…'

The man shook his head. 'There are three of us. The others are a bit further down the path, pretending to birdwatch. As soon as we set off, they'll follow.'

Becky looked at his rucksack and his boots.

'You'll find it easier in bare feet,' she said. 'And the rucksack will hold you up.'

The man nodded, took off his boots and put them in the rucksack. Then he stood up and heaved the rucksack onto his back. He saw that Becky was about to say something and stopped her. 'I'll need what's in here,' he said, shortly. 'We may be camping for a few nights.'

Becky looked at her watch. 'We'd better go,' she said. 'If we leave it any longer the tide will turn before we reach the island.'

The man frowned. 'But it's only…'

Becky broke in impatiently. 'You don't understand! It takes about an hour to get there.'

'An hour!' he repeated. 'It can't take that long! I can see the island from here.'

'It's very complicated,' said Becky. 'You can't just walk straight across the marsh. You have to keep doubling back to avoid the dangerous bits! Why do you think no-one else has discovered the way?'

The man looked at her and, seeing her tense face, he simply nodded and said 'OK. We're in your hands, Becky. Let's go.'

All along the edge of the marsh there were notices warning people not to walk there. Warnings of the treacherous bogs, the silt and the shifting sand that could suck you down. As Becky set off, she glanced anxiously up towards the coastal path. They would soon be out of sight but, just now, they were in full view of the walkers and she hoped no-one would try and stop them or go back to the quay and warn the coastguard. When she and Emma had made the causeway, they'd always waited until there was no-one in sight before they'd set off with their sacks of stones. But they'd have to risk it now. The tide wouldn't wait and they were already late.

And another thing – would she remember the way today, when it was really important. Not just for her, or even just for the Fieldings, but maybe for many other people. People who might be saved from ever trying drugs if they could stop these dealers. Becky pressed on, sometimes walking, sometimes running, frowning with concentration. The detective was always just beside her, and the other two men were close behind.

They'd already been going for about half an hour and they were taking much longer than she took on her own. The men's rucksacks were heavy and they couldn't move as fast as she could.

'We'll have to go faster,' she said, biting her lip. 'We'll never make it at this rate.'

She started to run then, jumping over creeks

and skirting muddy pools of seawater, slipping, sliding, never looking back but leading them on and praying they could keep up with her. She was confident of the way now. She'd done it so often during the summer when they built the causeway that it was burnt into her memory and, even though she was scared, her memory didn't let her down.

Behind her she heard the heavy breathing of the men, but she didn't dare stop. She looked at her watch again. They might just make it if they kept up this pace. She had a stitch in her side but she ignored it and kept on running, determined to get to the island in time.

Then at last, there it was just ahead of them.

94

But already the brick which marked the causeway was underwater. Becky would have to guess where it was. She splashed through the spreading sea to where the edge of the creek would have been at low tide and felt with her feet until at last she found the marker. Quickly she beckoned to the others.

'It's here! Opposite where I'm standing.'

The first detective lowered himself into the water, found the causeway firm under his feet and edged his way towards the other side. The second detective followed, but as the last one started off, he turned back and looked towards the mainland.

'What are you going to do, love?' he asked. 'You'll never get back now.'

Becky had been so anxious to get them to the island that she had not thought about herself. She had planned to race the tide back to the mainland, just as she'd done so many times before, and then meet up with her parents on the coastal path.

Helplessly, she watched as the sea swirled round her feet and started to fill up the network of tiny creeks which veined the marsh. Once the marsh was underwater, there was no way she could find her way back in safety. It was too late to go back now.

She looked at the detective and then she looked again towards the mainland. There was no choice. 'I'll have to stay on the island with you until the next low tide,' she said.

The man nodded and set off. The water was already up to his waist. Becky stared at the island. Then, still wearing her shorts and t-shirt, she lowered herself onto the causeway and waded across to the other side.

Chapter Ten

As soon as they were all on the island, they walked across to the shelter of the dunes, well away from the creek and the house-boat. It was late in the afternoon but there was still plenty of heat in the sun to dry out their wet clothes. They found a place between two dunes where they could set up camp and be completely hidden from view. As the afternoon slipped into evening, the men shared their food with Becky and afterwards as they sat and talked, she lay down and tried to sleep.

But she couldn't sleep. There were too many thoughts jarring in her head and she was too scared. What if the drug dealers came tonight? She was stranded here until the next low tide early tomorrow morning. If they came on the high tide tonight, she'd be here on the island with them! She sat up and hugged her knees. She looked across at the three men who were grouped together, a little way off.

'Are you certain nothing happened last night?' she asked.

One of the men raised his head. 'Certain, love. She's been there in that house-boat since last night and no-one's come near her.'

'What happens if they come tonight?'

The detective who had first approached Becky came and crouched beside her. 'If they do come, Becky, then I want you to stay right here, at the camp. You'll be quite safe.'

All through the long summer twilight, they waited. Every now and again, one of the men would check the time, but it was still too early.

Becky lay down again and she must have drifted into sleep, for suddenly someone was shaking her and a voice whispered close to her ear. 'We're off now, love. Wish us luck.'

Becky was awake immediately and she sat up. 'Have they come then?'

'No. But it's about the right time. We're going to move up behind the house-boat, so if they do come, we'll be ready for them.'

Becky nodded into the darkness and then the men were gone, swiftly and silently over the dunes towards the creek and the house-boat. Becky strained her ears but she could hear nothing except the distant slap of the waves on the other side of the island. She looked up at the night sky. It had been a cloudless day, but the weather was changing. There was a stiff breeze now and clouds were scudding across the face of the pale moon so that it only appeared infrequently.

'Perhaps they *will* come tonight if there's not much moon,' Becky muttered to herself. 'Perhaps they're waiting for a dark night like this.'

She had no idea how long she sat there, tense and silent. For a long time she heard absolutely nothing. Then she thought she heard the tiniest noise. She sat rigid, waiting to see if it would come again. It came again, no louder than the first time. Becky's heart started to beat faster. It wasn't the noise she was expecting to hear. She'd been expecting to hear the sound of shouts, of men's voices raised in anger. But this was quite different. It was something she'd heard before. It was the sound of singing!

She sat absolutely still until she was quite

certain that her ears weren't playing tricks on her. Then, hardly conscious of what she was doing, she got up and started to walk towards the sound. It was as though she was in a trance, unable to help herself. The atmosphere on the island was seeping into her whole body, just as it had before.

She climbed up to the top of the dune and looked over, careful to remain hidden from view. From here she should be able to see the house-boat and the creek, but it was too dark and at first she couldn't distinguish anything.

Then the moon came out from behind the clouds and, for a few fleeting seconds, the whole scene lay before her. She could see the police, crouched behind the house-boat. No-one coming to the island from the sea would be able to see them, but neither would they be able to see the drug dealers approach. The policemen knew this, but they had to stay hidden. This meant that they could not see what Becky saw, briefly lit by the moon.

A rowing-boat carrying two men had come in quite close to the island. One man stayed in the boat while the other got out and started to

walk across the dunes, through the shallows to the beach. As he walked, he took something from his jacket pocket, checked it, then put it back. And as he did so, it glinted. Becky had no doubt what it was. The pale moon had shone on the barrel of a gun!

Suddenly she realised what was happening. One of the dealers was going to check that the coast was clear, that Jake's aunt was in the house-boat and that no-one else was around. Meanwhile the other man would stay with the boat, with the drugs, ready to make a quick getaway if necessary.

But the police couldn't see this! As soon as the dealer got to the house-boat, they would surround him. They might catch him, but without the drugs, they'd never be able to prove anything!

Becky's mind froze. What could she do to help? If she ran to the house-boat now, everyone would hear her. If she crept round the way the police had gone, she'd be too late.

Then she heard the sound of singing again. It was closer this time and she looked round wildly to see where it came from. But there was nothing. Only the dark sea and the shape of the rowing-boat and the figures of the two men, one sitting waiting, and the other getting nearer and nearer the house-boat.

Then the moon went behind a bank of clouds again and everything was hidden. Becky stayed where she was, crouching, her heart hammering, knowing what was happening, but powerless to help. Who was singing? Surely not Jake's aunt? It was coming from the wrong direction. Could it be the selchie, trying to warn them all?

At last the moon appeared again but it was only for a few seconds. Becky looked down at the shore. There was silence, then, again the thin sad song. Becky strained her eyes, desperate to see if she was right, and this time she saw what she was looking for. Close in to the island a sleek whiskered head bobbed up for a moment, its sheen caught in the moonlight. Becky only saw it for an instant but it was long enough for her to recognise the Roman nose of a large grey seal.

Becky stayed quite still. Something, some instinct, told her to do nothing. If she moved, or tried to help, the spell would be broken and the seal would disappear. A few seconds more and the man would be at the house-boat.

Suddenly there was a shout, a curse, loud voices and the explosion of a gun going off. Then Becky moved. She crashed down the dune in the darkness, making towards the house-boat by instinct. But as she ran she heard what she had dreaded hearing. The sound of an outboard motor roaring into life, then fading as it headed out of the harbour.

'He's gone!' she shouted as she approached the house-boat. 'The one with the drugs has got away.'

One of the policemen stumbled out of the house-boat. 'Becky!'

'Out there!' panted Becky. 'The boat had an outboard motor on it. There's another man. I'm sure he's got the drugs on board with him.'

The policeman was quick to react. He darted back into the house-boat to get something, then he was out again.

Becky followed him and glanced quickly through the porthole. The soft light inside revealed signs of the recent struggle. The stove was upturned, food was scattered on the floor and blankets lay in an untidy heap. Jake's aunt was bending down, clearing up the mess. But the sealskin was nowhere to be seen! Becky felt the hairs on the back of her neck prickle with excitement.

On the beach, the policeman snapped on the huge flashlight he'd brought from the house-boat. He held it up and signalled. Two short flashes, then two long, two short again and then two long.

Becky rejoined him. 'What are you doing?'

'Telling the police launch to go after him!' he said, grimly.

'They won't catch him. He's got a long start.'

There came an answering flash from across the harbour and then bright lights and the sound of a powerful engine as the police launch roared off in pursuit.

'What happened?' asked Becky.

'We've got the first one,' said the policeman.

'Was anyone hurt?'

'No. The gun went off in the struggle, but no-one got hurt.'

Becky stood uncertainly on the sand with the policeman beside her. She felt flat and tired. After all this, they hadn't got the drugs. And without the drugs, the police couldn't prove anything. Unless...

Jake's aunt came out and stood beside her. 'Thank you Becky,' she said quietly.

'It didn't really help, though, did it?' said Becky. 'He's got away.'

'The launch may get him,' said the policeman, but he didn't sound very hopeful.

Then they heard noises coming from across the water. Suddenly there were more shouts and more lights.

'Look!' said Becky. 'The launch is coming back!'

They watched as the powerful lights of the police launch came slowly back towards the island. Beyond the sandbanks, the engine cut and someone shouted to them 'Are you all right there?'

'Fine. No-one hurt. What's happened?'

'We've got him. We've got the other one - and the drugs, too!'

'WHAT! How?'

A laugh drifted over the water towards them. 'It was a seal!'

'What! What do you mean?'

'A big grey seal doing a spot of night fishing. It upturned the boat. We'd never have caught him otherwise!'

'Well, would you believe it,' said the policeman, turning to Becky. 'A seal!'

Becky nodded. She believed it all right. And from across the water she heard again the faintest echo of that sad song.

Also in Puffin

WOLF
Gillian Cross

Cassy has never understood the connection between the secret midnight visitor to her nan's flat and her sudden trips to stay with her mother. But this time it seems different. She finds her mother living in a squat with her boyfriend Lyall and his son Robert. Lyall has devised a theatrical event for children on wolves, and Cassy is soon deeply involved in presenting it. Perhaps too involved – for she begins to sense a very real and terrifying wolf stalking her.

THE OUTSIDE CHILD
Nina Bawden

Imagine suddenly discovering you have a step-brother and -sister no one has ever told you about! It's the most exciting thing that's ever happened to Jane, and she can't wait to meet them. Perhaps at last she will become part of a 'proper' family, instead of for ever being the outside child. So begins a long search for her brother and sister, but when she finally does track them down, Jane finds there are still more surprises in store!

THE FOX OF SKELLAND
Rachel Dixon

Samantha's never liked the old custom of Foxing Day – the fox costume especially gives her the creeps. So when Jason and Rib, children of the new publicans at The Fox and Lady, find the costume and Jason wears it to the fancy-dress disco, she's sure something awful will happen.

Then Sam's old friend Joseph sees the ghost of the Lady and her fox. Has she really come back to exact vengeance on the village? Or has her appearance got something to do with the spate of burglaries in the area?

SKYLARK

K. M. Peyton

Life isn't much fun for Ben – until he meets Elf and is drawn into an exciting adventure. But the two children must keep their secret from the thoughtless adults in this delightful and touching story.

JEALOUS JOOLS AND DOMINIQUE

Sam McBratney

Many are the obstacles in the path of Jools's love for Dominique. Not least is Valroy, 'an alloy of several metals' and an interfering robot if ever there was one. The damage looks irreparable until Jools's eccentric Uncle Jerome steps in with some technical help.

ADAM'S ARK

Paul Stewart

Oscar's arrival in the house has a dramatic effect on Adam. In discovering that he can think-talk with the cat, he is at last able to make contact with the world around him. But the more he learns about the sad plight of animals everywhere, the more determined he is to discover why he alone has this extraordinary ability to communicate with them.